La Cucaracha Martina

Copyright © 1997 by Daniel Moreton

First published in 1997 by Turtle Books

Book & cover design by Daniel Moreton

The illustrations in this book were
created on an Apple™ Macintosh
using Adobe™ Illustrator.

for my
mom and dad
–with love

with thanks
to my brother,
Leo!

First Edition
Printed on 80# Mountie white, acid-free paper; Smyth sewn, cambric reinforced binding
Printed and bound in the United States of America

10   9   8   7   6   5   4   3   2   1

All rights reserved. No part of this book may be used or reproduced in any manner whatsoever
without written permission, except in the case of brief quotations embodied in critical articles and
reviews. Turtle Books is a trademark of Turtle Books, Inc. For information or permissions, address:

Turtle Books, 866 United Nations Plaza, Suite 525, New York, NY 10017

Library
of Congress
Cataloging-in-Publication Data
Moreton, Daniel.
La Cucaracha Martina :
a Caribbean folktale / retold and illustrated
by Daniel Moreton.   p. cm.
Summary: While searching for the source of one
beautiful sound, a ravishing cockroach rejects marriage
proposals from a menagerie of city animals which woo her
with their noises.
ISBN 1-890515-03-5 (hardcover : alk. paper)
[1. Folklore–Caribbean Area. 2. Cockroaches–Folklore.
3. Animal sounds–Folklore. 4. Noise–Folklore.]
I. Title. PZ8. 1.M815Cu 1997
398.2'09729'04525728–dc21
97-13631 CIP AC

**Distributed by
Publishers Group West**

ISBN 1-890515-03-5

La Cucaracha Martina

A Caribbean Folktale

retold and illustrated by Daniel Moreton

Turtle Books   New York

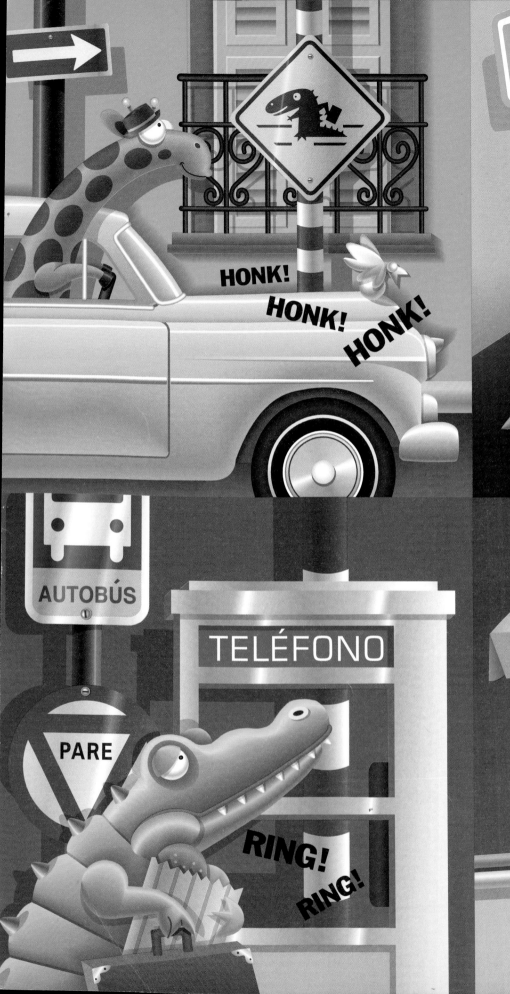

La Cucaracha Martina didn't care much for life in the big city. She didn't like the animals who hung out on the street corner and the thought of getting stepped on frightened her terribly.

KERPLINK!
KERPLUNK!

But it was the noise that Martina liked the least. The loud city sounds hurt her tiny ears and kept her awake at night.

On special nights, however, when all else was still, Martina would hear a *beautiful* noise, a soft gentle sound that came whispering through the night. It was the most fabulous noise she had ever heard and it made her feel all funny inside.

Early one Monday morning, La Cucaracha Martina decided to fix herself up and go out in search of the beautiful noise. She took some money over to the market and purchased—

a hairbrush

an eye pencil

a lipstick

three pieces of bubble gum

and

a big box of talcum powder.

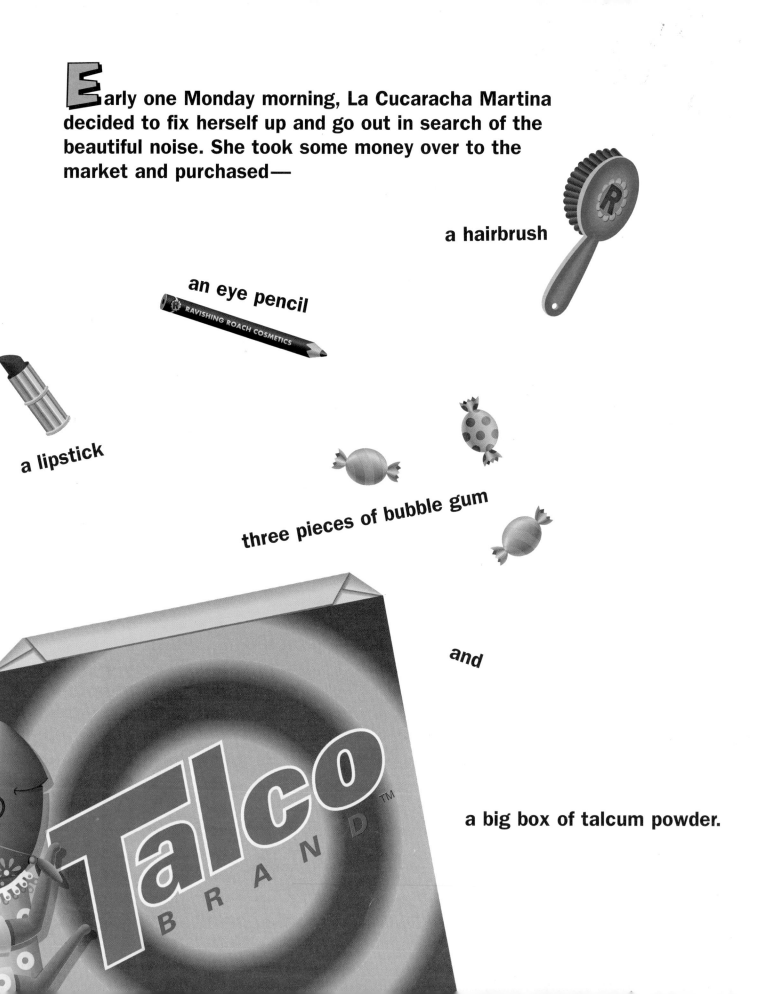

Martina worked quickly. She brushed her hair and fixed her face. She shined her shoes and buttoned up her best dress.

Never before had there been a more beautiful cucaracha.

By the time the noon whistle blew, Martina was out in search of the beautiful noise. She hadn't gone but one block when she was stopped by Dog.

"Good afternoon, Cucaracha Martina!" said Dog. "You look especially lovely today."

"Thank you,"
said La Cucaracha,
clutching her purse.

"Would you marry me?"
asked Dog smiling.

"Oh, I couldn't possibly,"
answered Martina. "I'm looking
for a beautiful noise."

"A beautiful noise?"
asked Dog.

And Dog went ...

OF! ARF! AARF! ARF!

"That's a terrible noise!" snapped Martina,

and she scurried off down the street.

La Cucaracha Martina
was well on her way,
when Pig suddenly blocked
her path.

"Excuse me!"
said La Cucaracha.

"No, excuse me!"
squealed Pig. "For you are
the most marvelous
cucaracha I have ever seen.
Would you marry me?"

"I can't marry you,"
said Martina. "You're a pig!
And besides, I'm looking for
a beautiful noise."

"A beautiful noise?"
huffed Pig.

And Pig went ...

REST

OINK
OINK
snort

Especiales
Arroz con pollo
Yuca con mojo
NO tenemos tortillas

"What a horrible noise," said La Cucaracha Martina, and she darted off down the block.

Soon after, Rooster came racing by La Cucaracha Martina.

"Pardon me, sightly senorita, you are a most gorgeous cucarachita," said Rooster. "Would you marry me?"

"I don't think I can, you see, I'm looking for a beautiful noise."

"A beautiful noise?" crowed Rooster.

And Rooster went ...

click click
click click
click
click

Not long after, La Cucaracha and Cricket moved away. They went off to the country, where a cockroach and a cricket could enjoy the sounds of silence. At night they would play bingo, make cocoa, and stare at the stars. And sometimes, on special nights, when all else was still, they would fill the night with beautiful noise.

cock-a-doodleee doodleee doodleee doo!

"My! That's quite a noise," said Martina, and she went off in search of the beautiful noise.

Rápido Rooster

Days passed and La Cucaracha Martina became the talk of the town. All eyes were on her as she shuffled down the street. Animals came from all over just to get a look at the ravishing roach in search of the beautiful noise.

PFFFT!

and Mouse . . .

SQUEAK!
SQUEAK!
SQUEAK!
SQUEAK!

and Bull
all the way from
Brazil!

m o o o o o o!

Weeks passed and La Cucaracha Martina thought only of the beautiful noise. No other sound would satisfy her . . .

not Fish,

GURGLE, GURGLE, glub, glub!

not Flea,

PEEP!

PEEP!

PEEP!

PEEP!

BUZZZZZZZZ

not even Bee.

Months passed and La Cucaracha Martina longed only to hear again the beautiful noise. She wanted to continue the search, but her six tiny feet could walk no further.

It was on this very night,
while getting ready for bed,
that La Cucaracha Martina
heard a familiar noise,
a soft, gentle noise,
a beautiful noise.

It was in fact *the* beautiful
noise! It grew stronger
and even more beautiful
until it filled the whole
room. Martina, beside
herself with joy,
stumbled over
to the window.

There, on the streetlamp below, was a tiny cricket making the most beautiful noise anyone had ever heard.

"Good evening," creaked Cricket.

"Good evening," sighed La Cucaracha Martina.

"You are the most beautiful cucaracha I have ever seen," serenaded Cricket.

"And *you* make the most beautiful noise I've ever heard," cried La Cucaracha. "Will you marry me?"

sang Cricket. **"Yes I will."**

And so they were wed....

Family and friends came creeping and crawling from all over just to witness this sensational sight. From Uncle Ernie to Aunt Hortensia, everyone agreed— the wedding was a spectacular success!